THE
GIRL WHO HAD EVERYTHING

Janice Greene

PAGETURNERS

Development and Production: Laurel Associates, Inc.
Cover and Interior Art: Black Eagle Productions

SADDLEBACK
PUBLISHING·INC.
Three Watson
Irvine, CA 92618-2767

Website: www.sdlback.com

ISBN 1-56254-702-X

Printed in the United States of America

09 08 07 06 05   9 8 7 6 5 4 3 2 1

CONTENTS

# Chapter 1

"Eww!" groaned the girl next to Alex. Worms were laid out on the tables. They were almost a foot long! Alex wrinkled her nose at the sharp chemical smell.

"You'll have to share," said Ms. Brennan, the science teacher. "Everyone please pick a partner."

Alex felt her neck begin to flush. No one would pick her—she knew it.

But then the new boy, Dave, walked up to her. He was as tall as she was. "Ms. Shaw?" he asked with exaggerated politeness. "I'd be honored if you'd share a worm with me."

Alex couldn't help but smile.

The students took their places, talking loudly. Next to each worm was a small knife. There was also a drawing of the worm's insides. It showed the body parts the students were supposed to find.

"Would you care to make the first cut, Ms. Shaw?" Dave asked.

"Be my guest," said Alex.

Dave poked the knife into the worm and began to cut. "It's slippery," he said. "Help me hold it, would you?"

Alex reached between his arms and grabbed each end. The worm felt like a noodle. A cold, stinky noodle.

"Nasty, huh?" said Dave. His face was close to hers. It was a nice face, with dark, shining eyes. She laughed nervously.

"I wanted to meet you," he said. "But I didn't think we'd meet over worm guts. Very romantic, don't you think?"

"Very," said Alex. She wanted to say more, but her mind went blank.

He smiled and her heart turned over.

Then he spoiled everything. He said, "Hey, I heard that you guys have your own plane? Is it true?"

Anger bubbled up in her. "Yes, we have our own plane," she hissed. "And I have five credit cards. And three TVs. And now I have something for you!"

She yanked the worm from his hands and threw it at his chest. It stuck to his T-shirt before dropping to the floor.

"Hey! What did I say?" Dave's face was shocked and angry.

Alex marched from the room.

"Alexandra—" Ms. Brennan's voice was a warning.

"Excuse me, Ms. Brennan," said Alex. "I'm about to throw up."

She hid in a bathroom stall until the bell rang. Girls came and went, hurrying out the door to the next class. Alex sat. She wasn't coming out until school was over. Of course, she'd get another pink slip. Two more pink slips and she'd be suspended. Her dad would be furious. So what? That would be great.

After the last bell, she waited. She wasn't going to let anyone see her leave.

The bathroom door swung open and she raised her feet. She heard quick steps come toward her.

Then she heard a voice she knew very well. "Missy, you come out of there right now," said Jerrilyn.

Alex opened the door. Jerrilyn, her bodyguard, stood with her hands on her hips. Her face was a dark thundercloud.

"You are never, *ever* going to pull an idiot stunt like this again!" she said. "Is that understood, Miss Alex?"

"Yes, ma'am," said Alex.

They walked down the hallway. "When that bell rings," Jerrilyn went on, "you go out in front where I can see you."

"Yes, ma'am," Alex sighed.

A few kids turned from their lockers and stared. Alex looked down and wished the floor would swallow her up.

The red luxury sedan was waiting out front. It was bright as a flag in the Los Angeles sun. Alex sank into the soft leather seat and slammed the door.

Jerrilyn turned up the AC and pulled smoothly away from the curb. "So tell me," she said, "what were you doing, hiding yourself in there?"

"Getting away from these stupid kids!" Alex cried. "They're horrible—all of them! I hate this school!"

"Oh? These kids look all right to me," Jerrilyn said. "What do they do that's so horrible?"

"None of them are interested in me—just my money," Alex explained.

"Hmm. What it sounds like to me," Jerrilyn went on, "is that you haven't given those kids half a chance."

"Hey, Jerrilyn, you missed our turn," Alex said.

"We're stopping at Gaylin's," Jerrilyn explained. "Your daddy's giving a party tonight. He said you should buy yourself something new to wear."

"I don't want anything new," Alex grumbled. "And I'll be late for ballet!"

"Not if you're quick," said Jerrilyn.

"Jerri, Dad won't even notice if I wear something old," said Alex.

"Don't start, missy," Jerrilyn sighed. "We're going to Gaylin's and then we're going to ballet. That's the program."

"Yes, ma'am," Alex sighed.

"Now, cheer up, baby," said Jerrilyn. "Your daddy's gonna be home for you tonight. Hey, there's nothing bad about that, is there?"

Alex knew that her dad *wouldn't* be there for her. He'd show her off in her nice new dress. He'd introduce her to strangers. Then he'd leave her alone.

They swung onto the broad street and pulled up at Gaylin's. None of the shops on this street had large signs. They were some of the most expensive stores in L.A.

Jerrilyn gave the keys to the parking attendant. As they walked inside, there was a blast of chilly air and loud music.

"Good afternoon," said the woman who was standing just inside the door. "May I get you something to drink?"

Alex looked at the woman curiously. Usually, the salespeople were very classy. This woman was nicely dressed—but something about her looked kind of rough. Maybe she was the owner.

"No, thank you," Jerrilyn said. "As a matter of fact, we're in a hurry."

"Not a problem," said the woman.

They were the only customers. A man stood smiling behind a black marble counter. Alex marched across the thick carpet to a row of dresses. A bright green dress had caught her eye.

The dress was a slender sheath of lime-colored silk. It would look perfect next to Jerrilyn's dark skin. The color would make Alex look sick.

"I'll take it," Alex said.

"Why, don't you want to try it on?" the woman asked. She glanced at Jerrilyn.

"You can't buy that without even seeing if it fits," Jerrilyn said. "Go on, baby. You've got time."

The woman led Alex to a row of

dressing rooms. The man behind the counter was fiddling with some papers. In spite of the cool air, his face was strangely shiny with sweat.

The woman closed the dressing room curtain. Alex sat down and started yanking off her sneakers and socks.

Then she froze. Had she heard someone cry out? The music was so loud she couldn't tell for sure.

Then Alex glanced down. There was a five-inch gap between the bottom of the dressing room wall and the carpet. She leaned forward and saw someone lying on the floor! She lay on her stomach and peered into the front showroom.

A woman's body was sprawled out sideways. It was Jerrilyn! Wide tape covered her mouth. An ugly purple bruise was on her forehead. Her eyes were huge with fright.

 **Chapter 2**

Gasping for breath, Alex scrambled to her feet. She hoped the background music in the store would cover any sound she had made.

She peeked through the curtain. Sure enough, Jerrilyn was face down on the showroom floor—not moving. Alex's hand trembled as she reached into her purse. Where was her cell phone? But the man and woman were already hurrying toward the dressing rooms. There was no time! She flung her purse over her shoulder.

A back door—there must be some place to unload a truck. She dashed by the next dressing room just as the man and woman came into sight. Alex ran. At the back of the store she spotted a wide door. To one side was a bathroom. Alex noticed several bottles and cans of cleaning products. She grabbed a bottle of window cleaner and shoved it in her purse.

She heard heavy footsteps coming up behind her. The man was breathing heavily and the woman was swearing loudly.

The padlock on the back door wasn't fastened. Now the man was just three feet behind her. Alex snatched the padlock and threw it hard at him. A snarl of pain told her she'd hit him.

She pulled open the door and sprang out into the sunshine. What should she do now? Where should she go? Seeing that a metal ladder ran up to the roof, she started climbing. The hot metal burned her fingers and bare feet.

When she reached the top, Alex looked around for a moment, panting. Then, she stepped to the side of the roof and looked down at the street below. The sidewalk was empty. "Will someone help me?" she screamed. *"Help!"*

The traffic flowed by. A woman in a convertible slowed and looked around. *"Up here!"* Alex yelled. But the man and woman from the store had now reached the top of the ladder.

Alex saw that the adjacent roof was five, maybe six feet away. She had often made five-foot jumps in her ballet classes. But what if it was farther than it looked? Her stomach tightened and turned cold. She backed up. The man was closing in on her, reaching out to grab at her waist. Alex swerved away from him and pushed off the edge. For a split second, she felt the rush of empty air around her. Her legs stretched wide in a nearly perfect jump.

Then she smacked down hard on the adjacent roof. Bits of tar and hot gravel scraped her bare feet. She turned and looked back to the other building. The man was gone. *The leap must have been too far for him. I've got to keep going.* Then Alex heard someone calling her name. It was coming from below. She looked over the roof's edge and was stunned to see Jerrilyn standing in the alley that Alex had just cleared.

"Alex!" Jerrilyn called again. "Come on! We can get to the car from here."

Alex stared at Jerrilyn. Just a few minutes ago, she had seemed to be unconscious. Now, she didn't seem to have been hurt at all. Alex continued to stare in silence as Jerrilyn moved to the roof ladder and began climbing.

Jerrilyn talked soothingly as she climbed. "It's okay, baby. I know you're scared. But I'm going to help you. Come to me, baby! *Hurry!*" Jerrilyn shouted as she reached the top of the roof and ran toward Alex.

"*You* took me to Gaylin's," Alex cried out. "You must be with them!"

Jerrilyn gave her a pained look. Her voice was warm. "You're just scared, baby," she said. "It's okay. Look, you go down to the street first. I'll cover for you.

Go on now!" Her hand moved toward her vest pocket.

Alex whipped the window cleaner out of her purse. The spray hit Jerrilyn's wrist, making her pause. Then Alex lunged forward and sprayed the woman's ear and the side of her face. Jerrilyn let out an anguished roar. She reached out blindly, but Alex was already running.

She looked down when she reached the end of the roof. About ten feet below was a big dumpster. Beyond that was a small parking lot. *Maybe I can jump into the dumpster, climb out, and run out into the street*, she thought.

The dumpster was piled high with cardboard boxes. What was in them? There was no time to wonder. Letting out a high, thin scream, Alex jumped.

She landed with a *whump*, the boxes crumpling under her hands and feet. The impact had thrown her sideways, painfully twisting her right foot. Now the corner of a box poked her neck. Gradually, Alex pulled herself toward the edge of the dumpster. Her breath was coming in ragged gasps.

As she gripped the hot metal edge, two hands grabbed her wrist. It was the man from the store! He was small, but the muscles in his arms were as big as baseballs and his hands gripped her like iron. When she lunged forward to bite him, he slapped her, making her ears ring.

Now the woman was reaching over the man's shoulder. She was holding a folded rag in her hand.

Alex thrashed and yelled, but she couldn't get away. The woman clapped the rag over her mouth. It smelled awful. Almost immediately, soft gray spots began to appear in front of Alex's eyes. They grew larger. She could still see Jerrilyn—her bodyguard and only friend in the world—standing behind the man. Alex tried to yell, *"I hate you!"* but everything had turned black.

Chapter 3

It must have been something they'd put in the rag. Her dreams were crazy. Alex dreamed that her mother was alive. She'd gotten out of the hospital bed and said, "The tumor's gone, Alex. It's your turn to get in bed."

Then Alex was on a ride called the Tilt-a-Whirl at the fair. She was alone in the car as it jerked her back and forth, back and forth. "Stop! Let me off!" she yelled. But no one heard her.

She opened her eyes to complete darkness. She was in the back of a panel truck. Every time it stopped, she rolled.

Now Alex noticed that her hands and back and neck were very sore. Her feet were raw. Her head throbbed painfully.

Worse than her pain, though, was the betrayal of her bodyguard. Jerrilyn had always been there. She'd made Alex do her homework and told her which jeans looked best. She'd listened. Now Alex had no one. She'd never felt so alone and afraid. Heavy sobs shook her. She cried for a long time.

Something rolled into her back—a bottle. She felt around in the dark and found more bottles, some clothes, and dirty fast-food containers. Alex was so hungry they almost smelled good. She pushed the junk to one end of the van. Then she piled up some clothes and lay down on them.

She had to make herself think. Her kidnappers wanted money—Daddy's money. So they wouldn't want her dead. That gave her a small advantage. Maybe she could escape after all.

At last, the truck stopped. When the back door opened, Alex could smell the ocean. The man climbed in.

"We're getting out," he said. "You're gonna follow Brandy. And I'll be right behind you, so don't get stupid."

She stepped out into a parking lot. The evening light seemed bright after the dark truck. No one else was around.

"Get her shoes," the woman snapped.

"Nah, leave her shoes, Brandy. She doesn't need shoes," Tick said.

Brandy's voice was cold. "Her feet are bleeding," she snarled. "Do you want bloodstains all over the place?"

Tick grunted and ran his hand through his thin hair.

Brandy gave him a hard look. "Don't mess up again," she said as Tick went back to the truck.

Beyond the parking lot Alex saw a few buildings and rundown stores. A wooden pier led out to the water. On either side were boats of all sizes.

Several people were on the walkway. Maybe if Alex ran and yelled—

Tick handed Alex her shoes and they

walked on. "I've got a gun here in my pocket," Tick said. "You try anything cute and I'll use it, I promise you. You'll never dance again, girl."

Alex felt a cold chill. They wouldn't kill her—but they could cripple her. And they knew that she danced ballet. Only Jerrilyn could have told them how much it meant to her.

It was a beautiful evening with a turquoise sky. Gulls swooped and dove around them. On one boat, a family was having dinner. One of the kids laughed, and the others joined in. Their laughter rang sweetly in the evening air. Alex felt like she was watching them through the bars of a prison.

Brandy stopped in front of a dingy white boat. It looked about 24 feet long. Years ago, it probably had been a handsome craft. Now, its wood was gray and peeling and its metal was rusted. Faded letters on the side of the boat spelled the proud name *Paradise*.

Brandy opened the hatch. Just below, Alex could see a metal ladder and a small space. "Get in," Brandy ordered.

Alex climbed down the ladder, and Brandy went after her. As they reached the bottom, Brandy grabbed Alex's shoulder. Then she slapped Alex so hard that her head snapped back.

"That's for making us chase after you!" she cried angrily.

And then she left, pulling the hatch shut behind her.

Alex sank to the floor. Tears stung her eyes. *Don't cry*, she told herself. *Crying will only make you tired.* She knew she had to keep her strength.

In a few minutes, she heard a motor start up. The boat began to vibrate and move. Tick opened the hatch and dropped down a little bag of chips, a small bag of cookies, and a bottle of soda. *Junk food*, thought Alex. Her ballet teacher, Ms. Montoya, would have a fit. Alex ate it all.

She looked around the hold. It was about ten feet long and so narrow she could touch both walls at once. Most of the space was taken up by a mattress covered with a sheet. There was a small lamp with a plastic shade and a tiny bathroom at one end.

Alex could imagine the plans Brandy and Tick had for her. They'd take her somewhere and make a deal with her dad. Then she'd be exchanged for her dad's money. His money would buy her life. And she'd owe him—oh, would she owe him. *No!* she told herself angrily. She refused to owe the man anything. She'd escape, no matter what.

As Alex looked at the lamp, she remembered a story of her mother's. When Mom was in college, her roommate had accidentally started a fire. The girl had tried to dry a T-shirt by draping it over a lamp. A few minutes later, though, the shirt had started to smoke!

Alex got a towel from the bathroom

and put it over the lamp. Then she went in the bathroom and soaked another towel with water. The sink was the size of a salad bowl. She spilled a lot of water.

Alex watched as a black spot appeared on the towel. Soon the smoke began to rise until it filled the room like a gray cloud. *"Fire!"* she screamed. *"Get me out of here!"* Then she quickly clapped the wet towel over her mouth.

Tick came charging down the ladder with a fire extinguisher. He sprayed wildly, hitting the ceiling and walls.

Alex waited in the bathroom. She could hear Tick coughing and choking. She knew he couldn't see her.

In a flash she charged past him, up the ladder. She didn't see Brandy.

Lights on the pier looked about a mile away. She could make it!

She took two steps toward the side. Then Brandy called out, "Don't you move!"—and she fired a gun over Alex's head.

Chapter 4

Alex froze.

With her gun still trained on Alex, Brandy was standing on the upper deck. "Sit down!" she yelled. Alex obeyed.

Brandy stared at her coldly. "Now you're going to get it," she hissed.

Gray smoke billowed out of the hold. Brandy yelled down to Tick, "Put out that fire and get up here!"

A few minutes later, Tick climbed on deck. He was coughing hard, and his eyes were red and wet. He sat down on a rickety deck chair.

For a minute, he couldn't talk. Then, between coughs, he said, "I put the fire out, but the smoke's still pretty bad. My throat's on fire."

Suddenly Brandy swore. A boat was headed their way. She pointed the gun at Alex. "Get in the hold," she snapped.

"Please!" said Alex. "I'll suffocate!"

"She might," Tick said.

"Shut up, Tick," Brandy hissed. "Alex, get down there and we'll leave the hatch open." She leaned close to Alex. The skin on her face looked rough and loose. Her green eyes narrowed angrily. "One peep out of you and you'll wish you were never born," she said.

Alex went partway down the ladder and listened. She kicked off her shoes.

A man's voice called out. "Hey! I saw the smoke. You guys need some help?"

"Thanks, but we're okay!" Brandy called back to him. "We put it out!"

The voice sounded closer. "Are you sure everything's all right?"

"Yes!" Brandy answered. "Everything's fine." Then she said, "Tick, get moving."

Tick was still coughing. "I need a drink," he groaned.

Brandy's voice was sarcastic. "Sure, go get yourself a nice drink," she said. "We've got all the time in the world."

Alex peeked out onto the deck. Tick was still slumped in the deck chair, coughing. Brandy was at the wheel.

"We're okay! Thanks!" She said with a wave. Then she started turning the boat in the opposite direction.

Now! thought Alex.

She rushed onto the deck. "Hey!" Tick yelled. But Alex was too fast. She dashed past him and jumped overboard.

She paddled furiously toward the other boat. *"Hey!"* she yelled. *"Help!"*

But the other boat had already turned around. It roared away.

Behind her, Alex could see the *Paradise* coming up fast. She took a huge breath and dove underwater.

She stayed under, counting to 60. Then she came up for air, hoping the waves would hide her.

It was getting dark. Good! Every

minute made it easier for her to hide.

She swam back toward the *Paradise*. When she came up for air, she could hear the engine close by. The boat was moving slowly now. A flashlight beam scanned the water. Alex ducked under again and dove deeply. She saw the propeller blades whirling under the boat and made sure to stay clear of them.

Alex came up on the other side of the *Paradise*. She could hear voices, but she couldn't make out the words. Tick's voice sounded hoarse and excited. Brandy's voice was low and mean.

Another flashlight beam. Alex ducked beneath the water's surface. She moved right up next to the boat, looking for something to hold onto.

She saw a metal loop with rope wound around it. Alex waited until the flashlight beam swung away from her. Then she pulled herself up to the side of the boat. Now she could see Tick's and Brandy's backs. Brandy was waving the flashlight back and forth over the water.

"Don't turn around," Alex whispered. She grabbed the end of the rope and pulled. It came loose all at once. She splashed back down in the water.

Again she dove deeply. She wondered if they'd heard her splash. After staying down as long as she could, she rose up and caught her breath. She listened. She could hear their voices, but they weren't close. *Good*, she thought. The end of the rope dangled in the water. *Very good.* Now she had something to hold onto! She decided to rest until they stopped looking for her. Then she'd swim to shore.

Alex held on. Now her wet clothes felt heavy and she was getting tired and hungry. But luckily, the water was cool, not cold. She could wait.

Suddenly, the voices were very close. Tick was whining. "I'm hungry. How long is this going to take?"

"As long as it takes," Brandy said in a nasty, irritated voice.

"Let's go. I'm sure she's drowned by now," Tick said.

"Shut up!" Brandy snapped as she directed the flashlight across the water.

"This is like looking for a bat in a coal mine," Tick whined.

Brandy's voice was harsh. "I said, shut up."

Then the light and the voices faded.

Alex looked at the lights on shore. It was a long swim, but she thought she could make it. Her dad had probably called the police by now, or maybe he'd even hired detectives.

But she was determined to make it home on her own. She didn't need him. She'd get to shore and knock on someone's door. One of those faraway lights must be a friendly place. Then she could call the police, and they'd take care of everything. She pictured Brandy and Tick in handcuffs. The thought was sweet.

Suddenly, Tick yelled. "There she is!"

Alex's eyes opened wide. She could hear Brandy's voice answering him, but she couldn't make out the words.

The boat slowly moved forward.

Alex was nervous. She wondered what in the world Tick had seen.

Then the *Paradise* stopped. Alex could hear the motor idling.

Finally, Alex couldn't stand it any longer. She pulled herself up and looked. Brandy and Tick were bent over the side of the boat. Brandy held the flashlight. Tick had a metal pole in his hands and was pulling hard. The muscles in his arms stood out like ropes.

"I don't know," he gasped. "It feels like she weighs a ton, at least."

"That's why they call it dead weight, genius," Brandy said.

"Okay, you don't have to be such a smart mouth, Brandy!" Tick complained.

Alex started to lower herself back down. As she did, a bright gleam caught her eye. Something was shining in the dim light of the cabin. It was Tick's gun, lying on the chair!

Slowly and silently, Alex hauled herself up onto the deck.

She watched as Brandy put the flashlight down and helped Tick with the pole. Both of them grunted and swore.

Alex slowly moved across the deck. She reached the chair. The pistol was cold and heavy in her hands. She tried to hold it still as she got ready to make her move. Every breath seemed to shake her.

Then Brandy grabbed the flashlight and looked down in the water. "You fool, it's just an old sleeping bag!" she screamed.

"Put your hands in the air—both of you!" Alex cried out.

Chapter 5

Brandy and Tick turned toward her. Tick's mouth hung open, and his eyes were blank with surprise. Brandy's mouth was creased in a hard, straight line.

"You're taking the boat to shore now," Alex said to Tick.

Tick started to move forward, but Brandy put out her hand to block his way. Her eyes never left Alex's face. "Give me the gun," she said.

Don't look at her, Alex told herself. "Hurry up!" she ordered Tick.

Brandy took a step forward.

"Don't move!" Alex said as she pointed the gun at Brandy's chest.

Brandy took another step forward. "Give me the gun," she said. Her voice was as cold as stone.

"Stop right there!" Alex cried.

Brandy kept moving.

"Take it easy, Brandy," Tick warned.

"I'll shoot you!" Alex cried out. Her voice was high and thin.

Brandy came closer. *Now!* Alex told herself. *Now! Stop her!*

The weight of the pistol seemed to grow heavier in her hand.

"Who are you kidding?" Brandy scoffed. "You're not going to shoot me."

Alex's finger stiffened on the trigger. She felt tears on her cheeks. Brandy slowly stretched out her hand.

Then suddenly, with one quick move, Brandy snatched the gun. Alex felt a rush of relief and shame as Tick lunged forward and grabbed her arms.

"That's it," Tick said. "I'm gonna shoot her in the foot. I'll mess it up good. Otherwise, she's going to try something, next chance she gets."

"You just hold her," Brandy said. "I'll take care of this."

Brandy slammed the gun down on Alex's shoulder. Feeling white-hot pain racing through her, Alex cringed. Yet she couldn't help noticing Brandy smile.

She wants power, Alex realized. *She wants me afraid.*

Alex screamed. It wasn't hard to sound scared. Then Brandy hit her again and again. Alex screamed and cried. Begging Brandy to stop, she swore that she'd never try to escape again.

When Brandy finally turned away, Alex hung like a rag doll in Tick's arms. He dragged her to the hold and let go. She half-fell, half-slid down the ladder and onto the mattress.

Soon Alex slipped into a pain-filled, dream-like state. Her mind wandered through the past. She remembered her mom watching her at ballet practice. Most mothers ran errands during practice sessions. Millie Shaw had patiently sat through every one.

Alex remembered the parties. One

Halloween, Mom had dyed a dozen sheets black. Then she'd made them into tunnels for kids to crawl through. They were hung with plastic spiders and cobwebs. For a whole day, she and Mom had decorated orange and black cupcakes.

For Easter, there was more than an egg hunt. She and Mom wrote directions to find the eggs. Mom made up riddles— really funny ones—for clues.

Nobody forgot Mom's parties.

Alex seldom saw her dad. Usually he came home after she was asleep. And he was often away on business trips. But it didn't matter much. Alex had always been her mom's little girl.

Dad made more and more money. First, there was the swimming pool and pool parties. Almost every weekend all summer long the backyard was full of friends. They sold the mountain cabin. Now, for vacations, they went to Paris or Bali. They moved to a bigger house with six bedrooms and four bathrooms.

Then, one day Alex came home and found her mom crying. She had cancer.

When Mom started taking medicine, her hair fell out in clumps. She got a wig that looked almost real. Alex hated it. For Alex's fourteenth birthday, Mom planned a garden party. She hired a ballerina to perform. But the day before the party, Mom fell and couldn't get up. Alex gave the cake and candy and sandwiches to the maid. To cancel the party, she e-mailed the guests. She couldn't bear talking to people on the phone.

Three months later, her mother was dead. More than 100 people came to the funeral. Everyone had loved Millie Shaw. Important people from Dad's business came, too. They looked smug and not at all sad in their expensive suits. Alex looked at them with disgust.

With her mother gone, Alex felt like an empty shell. There was a full-time cook in the house now, and a maid. Alex ignored them, drifting through the quiet rooms like a ghost. Friends came, but she didn't want to see anyone. After a while, they stopped coming.

She wanted her father, but he worked longer hours than ever. Once she was so lonely she called him at work. He let her talk, but she could tell that his mind was somewhere else. She didn't call again.

Dad didn't care about her ballet. He'd once said, "You can't make money dancing." Invitations to her recitals were mailed to the house. She tore them up before he could see them.

She did tell him about the man who followed her, one day after school. She'd called the police on her cell phone. After that, he'd hired Jerrilyn to protect her and drive her around. Jerrilyn had been a friend—before she was a traitor.

Alex couldn't trust anyone, even herself. With the gun in her hand, she'd had a real chance. But no. She'd backed down. *You're weak!* she told herself. *Weak like a puppy. Like a limp worm.* She started to sob, and then hated herself even more for crying.

Alex slept until shafts of daylight shone through the porthole. Now she could feel sharp twinges in her shoulder.

She found three small bags of chips lying at the bottom of the ladder. She ate them all. Then she shook every crumb into her palm and ate those, too.

Trying to keep her shoulder still, she lay down again. Suddenly, she was alert. Someone on deck was yelling—Brandy.

Alex climbed partway up the ladder and listened. Over the chugging of the motor, she heard the words "motel" and "Jerrilyn."

Alex's mind whirled. Had she really heard Jerrilyn's name? What did it mean?

Chapter 6

Alex wondered what was happening. Maybe her father was meeting Tick and Brandy at a motel to hand over a lot of money for her return.

And where did Jerrilyn fit in the picture? If she'd helped them kidnap her, she must be getting some of that money. Just thinking about that still hurt. Alex had always believed that Jerrilyn cared about her. *Guess not*, she thought bitterly.

Determined to hear the conversation, Alex wadded up several feet of toilet paper and wet it under the tap.

The next time Tick came down to the bathroom, she was ready. As soon as the door shut, she quietly climbed the ladder. Then she wedged the damp wad of paper in the corner of the hatch.

When Tick came out of the bathroom, Alex said, "I'm hungry!"

"Tough luck," Tick grunted.

"That was only about two handfuls of chips," she insisted. "I'm *starving*!"

"Quit your bellyaching!" Tick snarled as he started up the ladder. "Bad enough I get it from her. Now *you're* starting in on me. You females got to learn to shut up once in a while!"

He slammed the hold shut. Or *was* it shut? Alex waited a few minutes, then climbed up the ladder again.

The paper worked. The hatch wasn't completely closed. Alex reached up and slowly pushed it open an inch or so.

Now she'd be able to hear what was happening. Tick said, "You know what I'm gonna get first thing? A whole new set of weights. The ones I have now are secondhand, remember? And a big flat-screen TV. First class. This time it's gonna be first class, all the way."

Brandy said something Alex couldn't hear. Then Tick said, "Yeah? Why are *you* always the big genius around here? How about listening to *me* for a change?"

Then Tick moved away from the hold. His voice was drowned out by the motor.

Alex figured they were still making plans for the ransom money.

She wondered just how much Tick and Brandy were asking for her. A million? Two million? Their house had cost over two million dollars. Was she worth two million?

Alex could only catch a word here and there. Twice she heard Tick say, "Seven Palms." *Was that the name of the motel?*

Alex listened as long as she dared. Then she pulled out the wad of paper and shut the hatch. Tick hadn't noticed the paper—but Brandy might.

Once they reached the Seven Palms Motel, Tick and Brandy would call her dad and tell him to bring the money. But if the police knew she was headed there, they could show up first.

Alex surveyed every corner of the hold. She looked in the tiny bathroom. The medicine cabinet held nothing but an ancient tube of toothpaste. She peered under the mattress—bingo!—a dusty eyebrow pencil.

She sharpened the point with her fingernails and teeth. Then she pulled the worn-out old sheet away from the mattress. Using her teeth, she tore off a corner of the sheet and spread it on the floor. Carefully, she wrote: *"Please help me! We're at the Seven Palms Motel. Alexandra Shaw."*

She tucked the cloth into the waist of her pants and hid the eyebrow pencil. Then she waited, planning and hoping.

Moving carefully in the tiny space, she stretched. Suddenly, she longed for the ballet studio, with its wide smooth floor. She had a recital coming up in two weeks. But where would she be then? She wasn't sure she would even be alive.

As the sun slanted low through the porthole, Alex saw other boats. The *Paradise* slowed down, then chugged to a stop. Brandy swore at Tick as he tied up the boat. He yelled at her to shut up.

Then Tick opened the hatch and ordered Alex up the ladder. He leaned close to her, his voice low. "We're walking to the van," he said. "Now, you know what to do, right?"

"Yes, sir," she said respectfully.

She saw him almost smile. *So, you like respect*, she told him silently. *That's good to know. Maybe you even crave it.*

Brandy, who was putting on a jacket, turned and gave Alex a sharp look. "Now move!" she barked.

This harbor was larger than the one before. Along with fishing boats and sailboats, there were large powerboats and several yachts. Beyond the harbor Alex could see shops and restaurants.

They started to walk down the pier, Alex in the middle. Behind them, another group of people had also started to walk in the same direction.

Brandy leaned close to Alex. In a low voice she murmured, "The gun's here in my pocket and my hand's right on it. You just keep walking and don't get cute."

Alex could hear the voices of the people behind her. Guessing that they were 20 feet away, she kept her eyes straight ahead. Her face was blank. She hoped Brandy was watching her face.

Alex pulled at her waistband as if she felt an itch. The torn piece of sheet loosened, then fell. It brushed her ankle as she stepped away from it.

She hardly dared to breathe. Would Brandy notice? Would the people behind her see her message? Suppose one of them noticed it and called out, "Hey, you dropped something!"

They walked on quickly, in silence. Screaming seagulls circled above them.

This time there was no van. A dirty black car was waiting in the parking lot.

Brandy opened the back door. "Get down on the floor," she snapped at Alex.

The engine sputtered, then roared to life. They drove away. Alex moved beer cans out of the way so they wouldn't roll in her face. She tried to keep herself calm. Yet, every time the car stopped, she felt a little thrill of hope.

She hoped the motel was a long way from here. If someone had picked up her note . . . If they'd called the police . . . If the police were already at the motel when they got there . . . Oh, there was so much to hope for.

# Chapter 7

It seemed they drove for hours. Then at last Alex felt the car slow down, and Tick killed the engine.

"Get up," Brandy said roughly.

Alex saw that they were in a run-down neighborhood. They walked past a pawn shop and a dingy laundromat. When they turned the corner, she saw an orange neon sign: "Seven Palms Motel."

Alex's heart was pounding as they stepped into the lobby. It had once been a fancy place. Now, it was shabby. The cream and black floor tiles were chipped and broken. The bench under the window was stained, its leather cracked. A man with wavy gray hair sat there with a newspaper, filling out a crossword puzzle. A dusty plastic plant stood next to him.

From a door behind the desk, a bored-looking young woman entered. She pulled a cash box from a drawer and stared lazily at them.

"We need a room for the night," Brandy said. "Two beds."

"That's thirty-five," the woman said as she picked at the chipped nail polish on her thumb.

Tick started to fish his wallet out of his jeans. Then several things happened at once. The woman's eyes darted to the bench. The man's newspaper slid to the floor. The knob on the door behind the desk turned. The young woman shouted, *"LAPD! Freeze!"*

Brandy's hand moved like lightning. Before Alex saw what was happening, she could feel the gun's cold tip pressed hard against her head.

"Back off!" Brandy ordered. Now two more men were in the doorway. They, too, had guns drawn. Brandy gripped Alex's arm and pulled her around.

The gray-haired man moved toward them, holding a gun. His mouth was drawn in a tight line.

"Get back!" Brandy warned him.

"Just let Alexandra go," the man said, "before you get killed."

Brandy's voice was like iron. "Get out of my way," she hissed.

The man stepped back. He looked angry—and helpless.

Tick pulled the door open, and Brandy pushed Alex forward. "Look around outside!" she snapped at Tick.

Then there was a quick movement to their left. Alex saw a man duck behind a car. Brandy saw it, too.

"I've got the gun right on her!" she yelled in the man's direction. She pulled Alex forward. "Go!" she said.

They ran for the corner. Alex heard the whine of a bullet behind them.

Tick cried out in a yelp of pain. "I'm hit!" he gasped. "You drive."

"Give me the keys!" Brandy ordered.

Tick pulled the keys from his pocket. They were smeared with blood.

"Keep the gun on her!" Brandy said as they reached the car. She shoved the gun in Tick's hand and bent down behind him to unlock the car.

Tick held the gun to Alex's cheek. Across the street, two men were running low behind the parked cars.

"Get in!" Brandy yelled. Tick threw Alex onto the back seat, then scrambled in beside her. Alex's hands were shaking.

They took off into the stream of traffic.

"Look back!" Brandy yelled to Tick. "Are they following us?"

"I don't know!" Tick groaned. "I guess they've gotta be!"

"We're going to take the freeway," Brandy said. "We're heading south."

"No way!" Tick said. "They'll spot us for sure. They'll get a helicopter on us."

"Did I ask for your opinion?" Brandy snarled. On their right, Alex saw the sign for the freeway entrance.

Tick was terrified. "You're gonna get us killed!" he shrieked.

"Shut up!" Brandy screamed. *"Just shut up!"* They roared up the freeway entrance—and stopped cold.

A solid line of cars, moving about ten miles an hour, blocked the road. Tick swore loudly. Alex saw blood slowly dripping from the back of his hand. He didn't seem to notice.

Blaring the horn and waving her arm, Brandy forced her way to the inner lane. Across the barrier, traffic was moving faster in the opposite direction.

"Look back there!" Tick wailed. A police car was behind them, its lights flashing. Cars were trying to get out of the way, but they could barely move.

"You two get out!" Brandy yelled. "Run to the barrier!"

Tick opened the door and jumped out, pulling Alex behind him. Brandy released the brake and then scrambled after them.

With a loud crunch, the car hit the

SUV in front of it. The SUV's driver, a tall woman, braked and stepped out.

Tick, Alex, and Brandy climbed over the barrier. The hot night air blew grit from the freeway into Alex's face.

The tall woman yelled, "Hey! What are you doing? Come back here!"

Behind them, a cop, holding his gun in the air, dodged between the cars.

Brandy reached out to the nearest car. When she tapped the gun on the window, the car stopped. Alex could see the sheer terror in the driver's face. Brandy motioned for him to get out.

Tick pulled the driver out with one arm. He was a kid, not much older than Alex. His body was trembling. "Please don't shoot!" he begged.

Brandy got behind the wheel as Tick hustled Alex into the back seat.

Brandy took the next exit. "Tick," she said, "do something about your hand."

"Yeah, like what?" he whined. "Have you got a first aid kit handy?"

"Use your shirt!" she growled.

"You're all heart, aren't you?" Tick snarled. But he pulled off his shirt and wrapped it around his hand.

They entered a quiet neighborhood. The streets were lined with bungalows. Brandy parked the car and opened the door. "Let's go," she snapped.

"Why leave the car? It's a good car!" Tick said in a whiny voice.

"They'll find the car. They won't find us," said Brandy. "Now, *move!*"

They did. Dogs barked and a man yelled at them in Spanish as they ran through backyards. Brandy coughed and panted as she ran. Alex moved as slowly as she dared, hoping the police would catch up. They never did. Finally, they pulled up to an amusement park. The rides stood empty and dark.

"This way!" Brandy barked. They started to walk. Alex could see that Tick's bare chest was shiny with sweat.

Brandy led them to a brightly lit

street. "Bingo," she said under her breath. There must have been a dozen or more motels on both sides of the street.

Brandy stopped in front of a motel called the Lucky Seven Lodge.

"Stay put," she said as she walked into the lobby. "I'll check in."

Tick carefully unrolled his shirt from his hand. Alex grimaced at the sight of so much dark blood.

Tick caught her looking at him. "It's not too bad," he said. "See? I can move my fingers and all."

"You're pretty tough," Alex said.

"Yeah," he agreed. Alex could tell that he loved hearing that.

A few minutes later, they were in a big, ugly room with two beds.

Brandy turned to Alex. "You're on the floor," she said as if she were talking to a dog. She tossed one of the bed pillows down on the rug.

Alex could have slept anywhere. She lay down and closed her weary eyes.

Just as she was almost asleep, she heard a low voice—Brandy's. "We're not calling Jerrilyn," she said.

"Why not?" Tick asked.

"She must have been the one who tipped off those cops who were waiting for us at the Seven Palms," Brandy said. "Or else she messed up somehow. Either way—she's out."

Tick shrugged. "Too bad for you, Jerrilyn," he said. "Just too bad."

# Chapter 8

Alex woke to the smell of food and the sound of angry voices. She sat up. Tick was standing a few feet away, a fast-food bag in his hand.

Brandy was scowling at Tick. "You can't even get a simple order straight," she said. "Why did you buy so much?"

Tick said, "For the girl."

"You're not giving her two burgers!" Brandy snapped. "Give me one!"

"Come on, Brandy, don't be so mean!" he said. "She's a growing kid." He bent down and handed Alex two burgers.

Alex grabbed them and took a bite of each, before Brandy could interfere.

Brandy swore. In a fit of rage, she snatched up the remote from the TV stand and hurled it at Tick's head.

Tick ducked. The remote hit the wall with a loud *whack* and fell to the rug.

"You watch yourself, Brandy!" Tick yelled angrily.

She gave him an ugly look—so ugly it made Alex feel cold.

Tick pulled off his shoes and turned on the TV. After a couple of hours, Brandy got up and said, "I'm getting more food." She looked at Tick, as if expecting him to challenge her.

"Be my guest," he said calmly.

Brandy had been gone half an hour when there was a knock at the door.

Tick waited just behind the door, his gun in his hand.

A voice from outside said, "Open up. It's Jerrilyn."

Tick didn't make a move.

Jerrilyn's voice was louder this time. "You'd better open this door right now," she said, "or I'm calling the police."

Tick let her in. Jerrilyn looked at Alex. For a moment, her face looked like she was about to cry. Then she turned and faced Tick. "Where's Brandy?" she asked.

"Out," said Tick. "How'd you figure out we were here?"

"I know you've been trying to shake me off, you and Brandy," Jerrilyn said angrily. "If it weren't for me, you wouldn't even have her!" Then, without warning, Jerrilyn smashed her foot down on Tick's bare toes.

"*Auugh!*" Tick yelped.

He lunged for Jerrilyn, but she was too quick for him. Her hand snaked out and snatched the gun away.

Tick stared at her, gasping.

"Get back on the bed, Tick," Jerrilyn ordered. She turned to Alex. "Come on, baby. We're going home."

Alex sprang up and ran to her side.

As they went out the door, Jerrilyn said to Tick, "It was real simple to find you. And you can tell Brandy that seven isn't her lucky number anymore."

As Jerrilyn and Alex hurried away,

Alex said, "You *sold* me, Jerrilyn!"

Jerrilyn's face was full of pain. "That's the whole, ugly truth, baby. And if you never forgive me, I deserve it." Her voice broke as she went on. "What happened is I borrowed some money from the wrong people. When I couldn't pay it back I got desperate. But that's not an excuse. What I did—I did. And I'm gonna have to live with that every day of my life."

Alex reached out and gave Jerrilyn's shoulder a comforting squeeze. It was a solid, strong shoulder. More than once, Alex had leaned on that shoulder for a good long cry.

They reached the hot, bright street. "Where's the car?" Alex asked.

"I'm afraid there's no fancy car this time," Jerrilyn said. "Look over there. Those are my wheels."

It was a little car with faded red paint. Jerrilyn was putting the key in the ignition when they both saw a sudden movement in the back seat. *Brandy!*

Before Jerrilyn could push her away, Brandy had a thin, sharp knife right at her throat.

Brandy's voice was icy cold. "Give me your gun—now!" she growled.

Slowly, Jerrilyn pulled a gun from her purse and handed it back to Brandy.

"You got Tick's, too, or you wouldn't be here. Come on—" Brandy said.

"Okay," Jerrilyn said. She could feel the thin blade pressing against her neck.

"And I want your cell phone, too," Brandy barked. "Alex, give me her purse."

Alex handed back the purse. Then Brandy leaned toward Jerrilyn and said, "You're in luck, lady. I don't want to kill you here—not unless you try something stupid. Now you're just gonna drive away. Alex, you get out of the car and walk in front of me—go on!"

Jerrilyn's eyes were wet. "Good luck, baby," she said softly.

"I said *move!*" Brandy demanded as

she gave Alex a hard shove.

Alex watched the red car drive down the street as Brandy marched her back to the motel. "Good-bye," she whispered.

Brandy had a furious look on her face as she approached her partner. Tick was immediately defensive.

"Jerrilyn pulled a gun on me!" he said. "There was nothing I could do about it!"

"I don't have time for your excuses," Brandy snapped. "We're switching motels and then I'm making the call."

The call, thought Alex. *They were going to call her father.*

Chapter 9

An hour later, they were in another motel. This time, Alex noticed there was no "seven" in the name. The place was called *The Oceanside*, even though the ocean was miles away.

The room was much like the others—a thin-walled box. It had a TV, which was chained to the wall, two lumpy beds, and a tall, ugly lamp on the nightstand.

Brandy clicked on the TV and turned up the volume. Alex pretended to watch, but she was listening to Brandy.

"I have to go out now, Tick," Brandy said. "We need a car."

"I'll do that," Tick offered.

"Forget it," Brandy scoffed. "You'll just screw it up—like you always do."

"Such as when?" Tick's voice rose.

"Such as whenever you're awake!" Brandy snapped. She grabbed her purse and punched his shoulder as she headed for the door.

"You watch it, Brandy!" Tick yelled. "Don't make me hit you! You'll be sorry if you get me started!"

Brandy didn't even look at him. "Ha!" she said as she slammed the door.

They're mad enough to hurt each other, Alex thought. *Maybe I can do something to make them even angrier.*

After a few minutes, Alex turned to Tick and said, "How did you get the name, 'Tick'?"

"I was small as a kid," he explained.

"You're not small now," Alex said. "I bet you're much stronger than Brandy."

He snorted and looked proud of himself. "That's for sure," he said.

"How long have you two known each other?" Alex asked.

"About a hundred years," he growled.

"Oh, that must be why you're so patient with her," Alex said.

"What do you mean?" Tick asked.

"Well, she doesn't give you credit for being very smart," Alex went on.

"You got that right," Tick agreed.

"She really should be giving you more respect," Alex continued.

"Yeah!" said Tick. He slammed a fist on the bed.

Alex tried not to smile.

Then Tick turned on the TV and started watching a stupid game show. Alex tuned it out and thought: *If Tick and Brandy had a fight, maybe I'd have a chance to escape.* She remembered that night on the *Paradise*. When she'd pointed the gun at Brandy, she couldn't make herself shoot. Could she pull the trigger now? She wasn't sure. Yet she knew she had to stop them somehow.

Alex pictured Tick and Brandy counting money—and laughing. The thought made her grind her teeth.

Suddenly, the door opened. Brandy marched across the room and turned up the TV.

"Come over here," she ordered Tick.

Tick moved slowly. "So what's the big news, Miss Brandy?"

Then Brandy whispered something to Tick that Alex couldn't hear.

"You called them?" Tick gasped in disbelief. "They're coming here?"

"You fool! Keep your voice down!" Brandy growled.

"What a stupid idea!" Tick yelled.

"I'm handling this! So just shut up!" said Brandy.

"No way!" Tick objected. "We're getting out of here now."

Brandy laughed at him. "Since when did *you* start calling the shots, you loser?" she said with a sneer.

"Don't you *dare* call me that!" Tick hissed. The back of his neck was turning a dull, angry red.

"What's the matter, *loser*?" Brandy

taunted. "Can't you stand the truth?"

Tick pulled out his gun.

"Oh, come on," Brandy said. "Now, give me that." She snatched at the gun, but Tick quickly backed out of her way. He kept the gun trained on her chest.

"Come on now, Tick. Just give it to me!" Brandy ordered.

Tick looked very nervous—but also determined. His breath came fast.

Brandy's voice was quieter now. "Come on, Tick," she said.

Tick let out a long breath. Then he slowly stretched out his hand as if he meant to offer her the gun.

But Brandy was impatient. She suddenly lunged forward to grab the gun from his hand.

And Tick pulled the trigger.

Brandy's mouth dropped open in surprise. She clutched her stomach. The angry expression left her face. For a moment, she looked almost young. Then she flopped to the floor like a rag doll.

"Brandy!" Tick roared as he dropped to the floor beside her. "I didn't mean to, Brandy!"

Her knees shaking, Alex got up and moved slowly toward the lamp.

Gently, Tick turned Brandy over on her side. Her eyes were closed, but she still seemed to be breathing. *"Brandy!"* he called out again.

Now! Alex told herself. She yanked the tall lamp from the nightstand and charged toward Tick.

Tick looked up. But before he could focus, Alex swung. *Whack!* The heavy lamp base slammed down on his head.

Tick fell forward. Again, Alex brought the lamp down hard. But this time Tick grabbed the lamp base. Alex brought up her leg and kicked out at his chest. She put all the power from years of dancing behind that kick.

With a loud grunt, Tick flew backward and landed in the corner with a thud.

Alex sprinted away and threw the

door open. But at that same moment, Tick rolled on his side and fired.

Alex felt the bullet pierce her thigh. At the same moment a man who'd been waiting just outside the door pulled her out of Tick's range. Then three more men rushed into the room. "Drop your weapon!" one of them shouted.

Pain surrounded her like a red cloud. *My leg*, she thought. *What did you do to my leg?* One of the men picked her up and carried her away. Behind them, Alex could hear voices shouting and Tick snarling like a cornered dog.

She was carried out to the street and gently laid on the floor of an open van. She was shocked to see her father there. He bent over her and began to cry. Alex had never seen Louis Shaw cry before. Not ever.

Chapter 10

Alex heard the wail of an ambulance as she lay in the van. After that, she didn't remember very much. For hours—or was it days?—she drifted in and out of sleep, gratified that the pain had faded. Once in a while, she opened her eyes and thought she saw bright flowers on a table. But keeping her eyes open took too much effort. People in white came and went as she drifted in and out of consciousness. Yet whenever she was able to focus, her father was right beside her.

Then, one bright afternoon, Alex opened her eyes and said, "I'm starving!"

"Good!" Louis exclaimed.

Alex sat up and felt the dull pain in her leg. Her eyes instantly filled with tears. "My leg—" she cried out.

"Don't worry, honey, it'll heal," Louis said in a comforting voice. "The doctors say you'll be dancing in six months."

Alex breathed a long sigh of relief.

"You'll be in a cast for a while," Louis went on. "Then you can start physical therapy." He smiled. "You're young and in excellent physical shape. I know you'll work like mad to get back into ballet."

Even though it's a waste of time, right? she almost said. But she didn't. This was the best talk she'd had with her father in a long, long time. She didn't want to say anything that would spoil it.

Instead, she asked, "Where's Jerrilyn?"

Louis looked pained. "In the county jail," he said. "Alex, I'm terribly sorry about Jerrilyn. I'll never forgive myself for hiring her—for trusting her."

"Don't blame yourself, Dad," Alex said reassuringly. "I trusted her, too. And she *did* care a lot about me."

Louis didn't look convinced. "She claims that she tried to get you away from those terrible people," he said.

"It's true," Alex replied. "She felt really bad about what she did. She almost got me away from them. I should tell the police about that."

Louis tenderly squeezed her hand. "If that's what you want, sweetheart," he said. "Maybe that would help to get her a shorter prison sentence."

Then it occurred to Alex that Tick would go to prison, too. But Brandy— "What happened to Brandy?" she asked.

"That awful woman?" Louis said. "She's in the hospital. She'll live."

Now Alex remembered Tick pulling the trigger and Brandy falling to the floor. And she remembered herself holding the gun that night on the boat. *Okay, so I can't shoot anybody*, she thought. *Maybe I should be proud of that.*

Then the door opened and a nurse came in carrying a white orchid in a pot.

"For you, Alexandra," she said.

"Wow, an orchid!" Alex cried. She

reached for the card. It was from Dave, the new boy at school. The card said:

If you promise not to throw worms at me, I'd sure like to take you fishing on my boat this summer.

She smiled and turned to her dad. "It's from a new boy at school. He says he wants to take me fishing on his boat."

"Huh!" said Louis. "I bet you've had enough of boats to last a lifetime."

But Alex was touched by Dave's gesture of friendship. "Oh, I don't know, Dad," she replied. "It might be fun to give it a try."

"How about a trip with me first?" Louis suggested. "We could go right after school's out and you've done some physical therapy."

Alex was shocked. "What about your work?" she asked.

"I thought I'd take a leave from work, sweetheart," Louis said.

Alex stared at him.

Louis took her hand. "I almost *lost*

you, honey," he said. "That made me realize that I've been a poor excuse for a father. I've hardly seen you grow up. I've spent far too much time at work—especially since your mother died. The question is, do you want to spend time with *me*, Alex?"

Alex was amazed. "Can you really take time off?" she asked. "You always have such important deals going—"

Louis held up his hand. "I've got competent people at the office. I'm confident they can hold down the fort for a while. You're growing up. Soon you'll be out on your own. Spending some time with you matters more to me than anything else right now."

"Well, then—yes," Alex said happily. "I'd love to take a trip with you."

Her father's eyes lit up. "You *would*?" He looked like he could hardly believe it. She reached out to hug him.

"Thank you, sweetheart—for giving me a second chance to be a good father,"

Louis whispered softly in her ear.

Then he reached in his briefcase and brought out a fat envelope. Brightly colored travel brochures spilled out on the hospital bed. Alex saw pictures of mountains, beaches, cities, sunsets. Her dad looked as eager as a little boy.

"Now, Alexandra Shaw," he said with a big smile, "just where in the world would you like to go?"

COMPREHENSION QUESTIONS

RECALLING DETAILS

1. What was the name of the boat used in Alex's kidnapping?

2. Who owned the red luxury sedan described in the story? What color was Jerrilyn's car?

3. Whose death had left Alex feeling abandoned and lonely?

IDENTIFYING CHARACTERS

1. Which character was an accomplished ballet dancer?

2. Which character mentioned being very small as a child?

VOCABULARY

1. On a boat, what's the difference between a *hold* and a *hatch*?

2. Alex jumped to an *adjacent* roof. What does the word *adjacent* mean?